The Firefly Letters

A SUFFRAGETTE'S JOURNEY TO CUBA

The Firefly Letters

MARGARITA ENGLE

HENRY HOLT AND COMPANY

NEW YORK

Henry Holt and Company, LLC
Publishers since 1866
175 Fifth Avenue
New York, New York 10010
www.HenryHoltKids.com

Henry Holt® is a registered trademark of Henry Holt and Company, LLC.
Copyright © 2010 by Margarita Engle
All rights reserved.
Distributed in Canada by H. B. Fenn and Company Ltd.

Library of Congress Cataloging-in-Publication Data
Engle, Margarita.
The firefly letters : a suffragette's journey to Cuba / Margarita Engle. — 1st ed.
p.   cm.
ISBN 978-0-8050-9082-6
1. Women — Suffrage — Cuba — Juvenile poetry.   2. Young adult poetry,
American.   I. Title.
PS3555.N4254F57 2010   813'.54 — dc22   2009023445

First Edition — 2010
Printed in January 2011 in the United States of America
by R.R. Donnelley & Sons Company, Harrisonburg, Virginia

3 5 7 9 10 8 6 4 2

for Curtis, Victor, and Nicole
with love
and for Reka Simonsen
with gratitude

Your Majesty . . . I can from Cuba, better than from any other point on this side of the globe, speak of the New World, because Cuba lies between North and South America . . . Heaven and earth, the people, language, laws, manners, style of building, every thing is new . . .

FREDERIKA BREMER,
in a letter to Carolina Amelia,
Queen Dowager of Denmark
April, 1851

Matanzas, Cuba

CECILIA

I remember a wide river
and gray parrots with patches of red feathers
flashing across the African sky
like traveling stars
or Cuban fireflies.

In the silence of night
I still hear my mother wailing,
and I see my father's eyes
refusing to meet mine.

I was eight, plenty old enough
to understand that my father was haggling
with a wandering slave trader,
agreeing to exchange me
for a stolen cow.

Spanish sea captains and Arab merchants
are not the only men
who think of girls
as livestock.

ELENA

Mamá has informed me
that we will soon play hostess
to a Swedish traveler, a woman
called Fredrika, who is known to believe
that men and women are completely equal.
What an odd notion!

Papá has already warned me to ignore
any outlandish ideas that I might hear
from our strange visitor.

I have never imagined a woman
who could travel all over the world
just like a man!

Mamá says Fredrika
does not speak much Spanish,
so we will have to speak to her in English.

Cecilia can help.
I'm so glad Papá
taught one of the slave girls
how to speak the difficult language
of all the American engineers
who work at our sugar mills,
giving orders to the slaves.

I am sorry to say
that Cecilia's English
is much better than mine.
She is just a slave,
but she does have a way
with words.

Translating is a skill that makes her useful
in her own gloomy, sullen,
annoying way.

CECILIA

The visiting lady wears a little hat
and carries a bag of cookies
and bananas.

Her shoes are muddy.
She asks so many questions
that Elena turns her over to me
because my English is better
and I am a slave
accustomed to the rudeness
of strangers.

When I ask the foreign lady
where she is from,
she points toward the North Star.

Can her native country
truly be as distant
as the Congo,
my lost home?

FREDRIKA

In all my travels, I have never smelled
any place as unfamiliar as Cuba.
Even here in the lovely city of Matanzas,
with elegant shops and ladies in carriages
waving silk fans,
there is always the scent
of rotting tropical vegetation,
a smell that releases a bit of sorrow,
like the death of some small wild thing —
a bird, perhaps, or a frog.

I am eager to see the city
and then set off on my own,
exploring the beautiful countryside
with my translator, Cecilia,
a young African girl
with lovely dark eyes.

With her help
I will see how people live
on this island of winter sun
that makes me dream
of discovering Eden.

ELENA

I find the Swedish lady's freedom to wander
all over the island
without a chaperone
so disturbing
that I can hardly bear her company.

I hide in my room, embroidering
all sorts of dainty things—pillowcases
and gowns with pearl-studded lace ruffles
for my hope chest.

Cecilia and I are not quite the same age.
I am only twelve,
but I feel like a young woman,
and she is at least fifteen,
already married and pregnant.

Too soon, I will reach fourteen,
the age when I will be forced to marry
a man of my father's choice.
The thought of marriage
to some old frowning stranger
makes me feel just as helpless
as a slave.

FREDRIKA

When I asked the Swedish Consul
to place me in a quiet home
in the Cuban countryside,
I expected a thatched hut
on a small farm.

Instead, I find myself languishing
among gentry, surrounded by luxury.

The ladies of Matanzas
rarely set foot outdoors.
Enclosed in marble courtyards,
Elena and her mother move like shadows
lost in their private world
of silk and lace.

If I'd wanted to endure
the tedious life of a noblewoman,
I could have stayed home
at Årsta Castle, where my mother
never allowed me to speak to servants
and if I wanted to greet my father
I had to wait
while a footman
rolled out a carpet
and a hairdresser powdered
my father's pigtail.

There is no place more lonely
than a rich man's home.

C E C I L I A

Fredrika's visit is touching my life
in ways I could never have imagined.
She has asked Elena's father
to give us a little house in the big garden
where the two of us can live in peace,
surrounded by *cocuyos* — fireflies —
instead of chandeliers.

Together, we walk over hills and valleys
to see sugar plantations and coffee groves.
We visit fields owned by wealthy planters
and tiny patches of corn and yams
that belong to freed slaves
who live in little huts
that look like paradise.

We ride across rivers in small boats,
carrying bags of cookies and bananas
to share with all the children, dogs, goats,
and tame flamingos
that follow us wherever we go,
begging for treats, and hearing stories
about the North Star.

CECILIA

The huts of the freed slaves
make me think of my lost home —
I remember a ghostly mist
rising over the river
after a boy drowned
trying to escape
from the slave traders.

The mist was silent
but the water sang softly,
telling its own
flowing story.

If I had known
that my father would trade me
for a stolen cow,
I would have run away

into the forest
to live in a nest
made of dreams
and green leaves.

FREDRIKA

Cecilia is a fine translator,
floating back and forth
between English and Spanish so easily,
yet I feel certain that she is homesick
for Africa, and sadly, she suffers
from the lung sickness.
Walking tires her, so we often stop to rest
in lovely places, beside stream banks
or at the small farms of free men
who used to be slaves.

When I ask Cecilia about liberty,
she lists the prices:
Five hundred gold dollars
would buy the freedom of a slave
who works in the fields,
but she has been taught the art

of translation, so she is worth a fortune,
and her husband is a skilled horseman
valued at more than a thousand
gold dollars.

Fifteen dollars would be enough
to purchase liberty
for their unborn child.
The price will double
on the day of its birth.

How strange the laws are
on this beautiful island where —
if not for slavery —
I could think of the palm trees
and winter sun
as true evidence
of Eden
rediscovered.

ELENA

Cecilia and Fredrika live
in a hut in our garden, but they dine
in the big house with us,
and I must say that the Swedish lady
eats like a castaway
right after the long-awaited rescue
from starvation.

Fredrika tells us that her mother
never allowed her to eat her fill.
She was expected to be as thin and graceful
as a ballet dancer,
even though her natural shape
is sturdy and strong.

Hunger drove her to steal
strawberry cream cake from the pantry.

Anger made her toss her gloves into the fire.
Once, after writing a poem about the moon,
she burned it, because she knew
that nothing she did could ever be good enough
to please her stern mother.

FREDRIKA

On the coldest, darkest night
of Sweden's long winter,
I used to dress up as the Queen of Light,
with pine branches and candles
balanced on my head.

I walked carefully
to avoid setting my hair on fire
as I carried the traditional gift
of saffron buns to my parents.
I was ravenous, but I was permitted only
to keep half of one spicy golden pastry
for myself, even though girls
in other, more humble homes
were allowed to feast
during that midwinter celebration
of hope for spring.

I knew that I could not survive
as a half-starved rich girl
for the rest of my life.
Roaming the world
has been my escape.

CECILIA

My husband is a young man
of my own tribe.
He was chosen for me
by Elena's father.
His name is Beni
and he is a postillion,
a skilled horseman who rides
the fancy mare that pulls Elena's
swift high-wheeled *volanta* carriage
down the cobblestone street
whenever Elena and her mother
go out to buy silk and pearls
for her hope chest.

Perhaps, if I had been free
to choose Beni myself,
I might know how to love him,

but he is a stranger,
and now that I am living
in a cottage with Fredrika,
I hardly see my husband at all.

Out in the garden
lit by *cocuyos*
I feel unattached
if not free.

I feel like a young girl again,
unmarried and skinny,
with a flat belly
that has never
known the kick
of an impatient baby
so eager
to be born
into this world
of confusion.

BENI

If I had been free
to choose my own wife,
I would have married the girl
I loved so long ago
before I was captured
by men with guns
who carried me to this island,
a world of noble horses
and human hatred.

I ride with my back straight
and my hands gentle
so my trusting mount will know
that I am balanced and alert,
a rider who will never allow a horse
to stumble and fall.

I cannot protect myself
from the sorrows of this world,
but I can guide any horse
that is placed in my care.

CECILIA

Fredrika tells me she was in love
with a country preacher in her homeland.
He asked her to marry him, but she said no
because she felt certain that as a wife
she would lose her freedom to roam.

Travel is the magic
that allows her to write
about the lives of women
whose husbands think of them
as property
instead of people.

Fredrika says stories can lead
to a change in laws.

I am glad that Fredrika
has chosen to write
about Cuba
and slavery.

CECILIA

When Elena visits us in the cottage,
we take turns leafing
through Fredrika's sketchbook.

Some of the drawings are pictures
of famous people Fredrika met
while she was traveling in North America—
poets named Emerson
and Longfellow.

Some are pictures of Fredrika's friends
in Europe: the Queen of Denmark
and a wonderful storyteller
named Hans Christian Andersen
who is in love with a famous singer,
Jenny Lind, the Swedish Nightingale,

even though he knows
that the singer will never love him.

There are pictures of slaves
in the United States.
Fredrika admits that, until she saw
the United States of America
with her own eyes,
she imagined she might find paradise
in the land of Emerson
and Longfellow.

Instead, she found the slave market
in New Orleans, with a schoolhouse
right beside it
where children were singing
about the Land of the Free
while, just outside
their classroom window,
other children
were bought and sold
or traded
like stolen cows.

FREDRIKA

Cuban fireflies are the most amazing
little creatures I have ever seen.
They flock to me at night,
resting on my fingers
so that, while I am sketching
and writing letters,
I need no other lantern,
just the light
from their movements.

I skim my hand across the page
while the brilliant *cocuyos* help me decide
what to write—there is so much to tell.
How can I describe this shocking journey?

I must speak of Cecilia's homesickness
and her lung sickness

and the way her baby
is doomed to be born
into slavery.

I must describe Elena's loneliness
and her longing for a sense of purpose.

Somehow, I must show my readers
the bright flowers and glowing insects
that make Cuba's night
feel like morning.

CECILIA

When we visit the little huts
where freed slaves live without masters,
Fredrika asks them if they are happy
even though she already knows
the answer.

I believe she simply enjoys the chance
to hear free men and women
describe their little farms
as bits of paradise.

When she asks me if I long
for my birthplace in the Congo,
I tell her that I miss my mother,
and I ask her to put my words
in her letters, so that others will know

what it is like
to be a slave
so far from home.

FREDRIKA

Cecilia has just explained
Los Cuatro Consuelos,
"The Four Comforts" required
by Cuban law
as consolation
for slaves.

They have the right
to buy freedom
and the right to marry
and the right to own property
and the right to petition
for transfer
to a new owner
if the first one turns out
to be cruel
or unfair. . . .

Of course, none of this seems
adequate or logical
because how can slavery
ever be fair?

When I ask Cecilia
if wealthy planters
honor these laws,
she smiles in a wistful way
that helps me understand
why my question
is foolish.

CECILIA

We go out at night
to rescue fireflies.

Children catch the friendly *cocuyos*
and pull off their wings
or put them in bottles
to make little lamps
where the insects glow and fly
until they starve.

Women tie living *cocuyos*
onto their ruffled dresses as ornaments
and girls weave them
into their hair
like flashing jewels.

Fredrika and I
feel like heroines in a story,
following people around
buying captive fireflies
and setting them free.

I notice Elena
peering down from her window,
smiling as she watches
us rush around in circles
rescuing hundreds of small bright creatures
from the sad fate of all
living captives,
even those
with wings.

ELENA

How disturbing it feels
to envy Cecilia,
a slave.

She is free,
at least for now,
to run and shout
out in the open
with Fredrika,
talking to strangers
and splashing
in mud puddles
just like a man
or a boy.

How I wish
that I could go out with them
tonight, to the beach!

In a moment
of hesitant courage
I ask Mamá
to let me venture outdoors . . .

but she scolds me for wishing
to have muddy shoes
and a chance to run
faster and faster
in circles
beneath the light
of the eerie,
dangerous moon.

FREDRIKA

Cubans believe moonlight
is harmful.
Cecilia covers her head
with a blue turban. She warns me
that I should protect myself
from the moon,
although she cannot say
exactly why.

The beach is so lovely
that I feel like a flying fish,
as if I am soaring
up into the starlit sky.

When Cecilia suddenly runs away
from a few small boats

that are bobbing on the waves,
I am perplexed.

How can anything
as beautiful as a moonlit night
be dangerous?

CECILIA

I try to warn her,
but she will not listen.

She jumps up and down
in the roaring waves
like a happy child.

The boats are close now —
I cannot stay!
The memory of arrival
and loss
is too fresh.

Fredrika does not see their faces yet,
all the children from a slave ship
riding in those small boats,

gliding toward this lonely shore
in chains.

I run and run
until my lungs ache
and I cough
and then I collapse
in the muddy road
that leads away
from the soft sand
of the beach.

Gasping for breath,
I struggle to remember
my mother's voice,
and I struggle
to forget
all the rest. . . .

CECILIA

I remember monkeys
swinging and screaming in the great forest
and a cobra swimming between water plants
in a river the color of coffee.

At sunset, the same river looked purple,
and in the morning it was green.
Light was the only thing
that had changed.

Now, on the far side of the world
here in Cuba—island of torment—
I wonder if light from my homeland
follows me at night, in waking dreams
where it is always daytime
and the river is always sky blue

and every sea breeze is sweet
and gentle
like my mother's singsong
lullaby voice.

ELENA

Cecilia asks me for help—
Fredrika has taken to her bed
with a sick headache
that goes on day after day,
for a week. . . .

I cannot believe
that Cecilia allowed Fredrika to watch
one of the secret ships
as it dropped its cargo on the beach.
Transporting slaves is forbidden
by a treaty with England—
that is why the price of each slave
is so high.

Even though ships from Africa are illegal,
Papá and the other planters

know how to keep them coming,
each with seven or eight hundred
new slaves, mostly children
who are less likely to rebel
or escape.

CECILIA

I remember wild animals
near the river —
crocodiles, hippos, and leopards
who made the night terrifying.

None of those beasts were as frightening
as people — the strangers
who came with guns
to seize children
or with goods
to buy children.

I do not remember
the ocean.

The distance
between then and now

is too vast for memory

or a calendar

or a map.

FREDRIKA

This island, with its lush gardens
and winter sun,
had me fooled.

I have always imagined
that a gentle climate would make the people
gentle too . . . but that is not the way
of the human heart
when it is lost in the selfishness
of greed.

If only I had known about the boats,
I never would have asked Cecilia
to accompany me to that same cursed
moonlit beach
where she arrived in chains
just a few years ago. . . .

In the eyes of Cecilia
and each enslaved child
I see
hopeful light.

FREDRIKA

By asking many questions,
I have discovered
that fifty gold American dollars
per child
is the price paid by planters
to silence the magistrates
who might otherwise cause trouble
when forbidden ships
bring new captives
to quiet beaches
under the radiant
dangerous moon.

No wonder Cecilia told me to cover my head
so that I would have a cloth to wipe my eyes
after witnessing a sorrow so great
that I must now think carefully

about how to describe slavery
in such a way
that my true stories
about Cuba
will be believed.

CECILIA

After a weeklong headache,
Fredrika is finally feeling stronger,
so we go out again, at night,
to rescue *cocuyos*.

The insects eventually grow weary of flying
and return to earth
where they are captured again,
so we have to rescue the same fireflies
over and over,
buying them from greedy children
who think we are playing a game.

When Fredrika runs out of pennies,
she spends cookies and bananas
until she is left with nothing to trade

and cannot help the fireflies who remain prisoners
too numerous to save.

Even though we can never help them all,
I feel my mind flying and glowing
along with the winged creatures
that we have rescued
as they soar away, free. . . .

ELENA

Once again, I watch from the window
while Fredrika and Cecilia
run wildly in circles
setting *cocuyos* free.

A harpist comes to the window,
offering to serenade me
for a price.

I have never possessed
any coins of my own,
so I give him an embroidered
linen handkerchief
that he can trade for coins or food.

After playing three songs,
he strolls away, and I wonder

if anyone will ever
serenade me
for love
instead of money.

ELENA

I sit with a row of slave women,
teaching them how to sew.

When they do extra work
on Sunday afternoons,
they can earn a bit of money
to save toward buying their freedom
from Papá.

If Mamá would allow me,
I would even teach them how to read
and paint, and play music on the piano.

Artisans and musicians
are well-paid,

the slaves most likely
to earn enough money
for liberty's
steep price.

CECILIA

Imagine my nervousness
having to translate while Fredrika
scolds the schoolmistress
for keeping girls in class
only one hour per day
and for teaching them nothing
but embroidery, lacemaking,
and saints' lives
while boys study all day long
learning mathematics and science.

Elena looks so astounded
sitting in her classroom,
surrounded by giggling girls
in silk dresses with lace ruffles,
while Fredrika scolds
and I translate,

all the time thinking
that one hour of school
is more than any slave girl
can hope to receive
in a lifetime.

CECILIA

In church, Fredrika kneels
in the back, next to the slaves,
instead of sitting up front
with the ladies who are draped
in silks and jewels,
with lace shawls on their heads
instead of turbans.

I kneel beside Fredrika
with my baby kicking
in my belly
while I pray,
wondering if babies
can hear voices
and the music
that pours out the door

of the church
and up
toward the blue sky.

BENI

With the Swedish lady
kneeling beside us in church,
I begin to wonder how much my wife
will have changed
by spending so much time
in the company of a stranger
from the land of the North Star.

I hardly know Cecilia.
We are married
but we are strangers.

When the foreigner
goes away from Cuba
to travel in some other
distant foreign land,

will she leave my wife
with useful gifts . . .
or just fine ideas
and wild hopes?

FREDRIKA

I gave up my wealth
when I left my father's castle
to roam, and to write.

Now, I am troubled by my inability
to help Cecilia buy her freedom
and the liberty of her husband
and her child,
and I am overwhelmed by my wish
to help all the other slaves
on this suffering island.

Even if I had thousands of gold dollars,
I could not give them to Cecilia
without offending my host, Elena's father,
and that would cause problems
for the Swedish Consul —

an international incident
between our two nations.

Still, I would do it
if I had inherited
my father's gold.

CECILIA

In the evenings
I look over Fredrika's shoulder
as she writes letters
with fireflies resting
on her hand.

When I ask her to tell me
what the rows of squiggles mean,
she reads her Swedish words out loud,
translating into English
so that I can understand
when she describes Cuba as one
of God's most beautiful creations—
an island of eternal summer
like an outer court of Paradise
where she has inhaled new life,
although she cannot imagine

having to stay here
and live in this garden
where freedom
does not grow.

FREDRIKA

The quality of light in tropical air
is more intense, and on hot days
a sea breeze feels like the breath of heaven.

I cannot understand
how people who live surrounded
by so much beauty
can shut themselves up indoors
like Elena, and her mother.

Can it be
that they are afraid
of hideous truths
that will be revealed
by the lovely sun
as well as the dangerous
moon?

E L E N A

Fredrika says her father
gave her a hill
for her birthday.

The hill was stony,
but it overlooked
a green meadow.

Her older sister
had received a hill too,
but one with gardens, walkways,
and benches for visiting
with friends.

Fredrika's hill had nothing
but a view
of wildflowers
growing.

C E C I L I A

When we go out at night
to watch the dances of slaves
on sugar plantations,
Fredrika sketches furiously
in her fat notebook,
turning the bursting pages
in a frenzy of excitement.

She says she loves the music of drums
and the graceful movements of dancers
just as much as she loves her own
treasured freedom to roam.

An overseer orders me to warn Fredrika
that some of the songs might be prayers
to dangerous spirits from distant jungles,
but Fredrika merely smiles, and tells me

that in Sweden people still believe in elves
and trolls, and a World Tree with roots
in the Fountain of Destiny.

I understand none of this
until Fredrika explains
that she has no wish to judge
the beliefs of others
because her own beliefs include
both the endless comfort
of the goodness of God
and the practical help
of a little traveling fairy
who rides on her shoulder
protecting her from harm.

I try to see a traveling fairy
on my own shoulder . . .
but all I see is Fredrika
at my side,
helping me to imagine
invisible wings.

FREDRIKA

Ships of stone in a Viking graveyard,
eerie Northern Lights
and golden cloudberries
gathered by little gray men
who guard the barns and cows —
the mysteries of the world are endless.

Once, when I was little,
I wandered away and got lost
in a wooded park
where I saw a forest spirit
playing music on his flute,
and later, after I had been rescued,
I told my father that I had met
the piping god Pan.
That is when my father decided
that I was meant

to be a writer.
He was not pleased.

When I asked my mother
to give me a room of my own
where I could be alone
to read and write poems,
she refused.

Writing was not considered ladylike
in a castle with plenty of room
for pianos and ballet.

E L E N A

The castle where Fredrika
spent her childhood
was haunted.

In the attic, there was a sword
that had beheaded a nobleman
during a war.

There were bloodstained clothes
beside the sword.

None of the servants would climb
up to the attic to fetch boxes or trunks
that had been stored
next to ghosts.

This house where I live
is haunted too.

It was built by slaves
who rebelled, and buried an overseer
inside the walls.

Papá has never been able to find
the skeleton,
but sometimes at night
I hear pitiful moans
and rattling chains.

It is either the ghost
or some poor child
from the slave ships
being driven
to market.

CECILIA

On one of our walks
we stop to rest on a hill
with a view of palm trees
waving in the distance.

Fredrika says she feels
like we have wings, and we are both flying
over the brilliant green earth.

Later, when we walk downhill
into a forest, we find ourselves surrounded
by trees that are slowly being choked
by strangler figs.

The strangler trees have branches
that wrap themselves like long skinny arms
around other trees.

Fredrika sketches sadly
while I wonder
what has happened
to our wings.

FREDRIKA

Cecilia coughs and gasps,
and I wonder if she needs fresh air,
so I ask Elena's parents to help me find
a simple home out in the countryside
where Cecilia can breathe clean sky
untainted by the smokestacks
of sugar mills.

Beni drives us in a carriage
that scurries over the hills
like a swift insect, or a spider.

Finally, we reach a thatched farmhouse
with a clean-swept earthen floor
and an outdoor kitchen
and the tranquil coziness
of a country home

where the people are poor
but hardworking
and filled with love
for one another.

Our hosts are peasants
from the Canary Islands,
a remote outpost
of volcanic, stony fields and vineyards
off the southern coast of Spain,
not far
from Morocco.

Our beds are hammocks.
The woman is up early
blowing a conch-shell trumpet
to call her husband and sons
in from the fields
for a simple breakfast
of fish, corn, and yams.

All the bowls, spoons, and cups
are made from gourds, the hard, dry fruit
of a calabash tree that grows near the house
along with every other variety of fruit tree
known in the tropics:
mango, sapote, mamey, tamarind,
and half a dozen different types of bananas,
some tiny, and others huge. . . .

It is a garden
of delightful scents
and enchanted flavors . . .

a garden that somehow
helps me revive
the old hope of rediscovering
lost fragments
of Eden.

CECILIA

My sore lungs find no relief
out in this wilderness
of dusty trails,
but I am happy to stay here
so far from the beaches
where ships deliver slaves
and so far from the mills
where vats of sugar
are stirred
like the brew of witches
in stories.

Fredrika plays with the children
who follow us constantly,
pretending that bunches of bananas
are clusters of little yellow chickens
peeking out from beneath

the leafy green wings
of their mother,
the banana tree.

I try to sketch
in Fredrika's notebook,
but my fingers are not accustomed
to copying the loveliness of brilliant flowers
and darting hummingbirds.

When the pencil breaks
I use a splinter of charcoal
from the cooking fire.

I do not care if my sketches
are rough and messy —
drawing pictures on wings of paper
makes me feel like an angel of God
sketching plans for the creation
of an entirely new world,
one without sorrow or pain.

Fredrika tells me that my eyes
are suddenly sparkling with hope.

She gives me a sketchbook
and a pencil of my own.

Suddenly, I feel like an artist
or a magician.

FREDRIKA

After a supper of boiled beans and rice,
Cecilia reveals that she has brought
a gift of butter and cake from Elena's home.
We eat with pleasure
in these peaceful surroundings
that make me feel like a shepherdess
in some ancient story of wisdom or magic.

There is no evening in the tropics.
Night simply drapes itself over the day
as if someone had lowered a curtain.
The sky glitters and moves,
filled with shooting stars and fireflies.

Out here, no one tries to catch
the soaring insects.

The *cocuyos* drift so high
that they seem to live in heaven,
like stars.

CECILIA

Blue doves and green parrots
surround us in the mornings.
Children play games at our feet.
This home is friendly and restful,
so why am I tired?

I cough until my lungs bleed,
making me wonder if the baby in my belly
can feel scared too, and sad — is the baby
aware of my reluctance to leave
this tranquil farm
and return to the life of a slave
at the mill,
translating for American engineers
as they shout at me in English
and I shout at others in a mixture of Spanish
and several African languages,

as if the entire world can be found
trapped inside one Cuban sugar mill
and trapped inside
my own voice?

FREDRIKA

I ask Cecilia to walk with me
toward the sound of drums.
We find ourselves following a long trail
to a distant plantation, where slaves dance
in front of the windowless barracoons
where they must sleep at night
in chains, behind locked doors.

I sketch the dancers
until an overseer notices me
and seizes my notebook
and tears out the pages.
He uses his whip to end the dance.
He chases me away, with Cecilia
at my side, coughing and weeping.

I am ready to leave Cuba,
but how can I go—how can I abandon
this sick girl who has worked so hard
to help me understand
this beautiful island
with its hideous ways?

B E N I

When I am sent to fetch my wife
and the foreign lady
from the remote farm
where they have been staying,
I notice that Cecilia looks ill,
and I begin to wonder
if she will live long enough
to be a mother to our child.

We arrive in the city
under stars.

Cecilia's head is uncovered,
and I feel angry
because perhaps my wife
has been weakened

by roaming with a foreigner,
her head unprotected,
exposed to the rays
of Cuba's moon.

ELENA

They are back!
Oh, how I wish I could have gone
with them out to the countryside.

I have missed them, and I have missed
the excitement of Fredrika's stories
about adventures in faraway places.

I have missed seeing her sketchbook
filled with unfamiliar views
of this island where I have lived
all my life,
without seeing much at all
beyond the four walls
of my own room.

I have even missed Cecilia,
with her strong spirit
and the way she whispers
a comforting lullaby
to the restless baby
as it kicks and rolls
inside her huge belly.

I don't know how or why
it happened,
but somehow
I have begun
to think of Cecilia
as my best friend.

FREDRIKA

I have decided to postpone
my departure from Cuba.
I cannot bear to think of leaving
until I feel certain
that I can somehow
offer help to Cecilia
and Beni
and their baby.

For now, there is the delightful prospect
of watching as freed slaves dance
to raise money
for helping orphans
of all colors.

Elena and Cecilia are both so excited—
they refer to the upcoming charity dance
as the Ball of Free Blacks.

They tell me that even the wealthiest nobles
attend the dance, and donate money
to help freed slaves
feed orphans.

CECILIA

Will I ever feel as free
as during those mornings
when I sketched banana trees
and wildflowers
on the farm of the Canary Islanders
where I felt like an orphan
in a story,
an orphan who has finally
been adopted?

For now, I am stuck
in the city
once again.

This will be my first visit
to the Ball of Free Blacks.

Elena gives me a blue satin dress,
and Fredrika helps me adjust the waist
to fit my growing belly.

If only Beni could attend too
and dance with me
at the Ball . . .
but my husband must stand
beside Elena's carriage,
protecting the valuable horse
from thieves
and mischievous children
who might try to ride
just for fun.

I have grown to admire
my husband's dedication
to the constant
protection and care
of each horse.

I believe he will be
a good father.

ELENA

Flowers, lamps, and ornaments
decorate the dance hall.

There must be three hundred people,
all fashionably dressed,
dancing minuets
and trailing garlands of roses.

Fredrika stands beside a table
loaded with bouquets.
She stares at a line of ants
as they carry flower petals
up a wall,
balancing them
like colorful umbrellas.

She does not seem impressed
with frilly dresses
and ornate dance steps.

I suppose she is accustomed
to all the luxuries
of Europe.

After the ball
we climb up to the roof of my house
to watch stars
fall from the sky.

Where do they land?
Are they really good luck?

Cecilia watches
with one hand on her belly
and tears in her eyes.

I imagine she must be wishing
on a star . . . wishing for her baby's
freedom.

CECILIA

Wishing on stars brings nothing
but disappointment.

How can I ever manage
to buy my baby's freedom,
and even if I could,
what would happen next?
Would my child grow up
ashamed of parents
who are slaves?

The ways of this island
are too confusing for me.

I just want to breathe
without gasping for air

and love my baby
without struggling
to understand
the impossible future.

FREDRIKA

The Ball of Free Blacks
reminded me of dances in Europe.
The dancers were stiff.
In my sketchbook
they look like lines of ants
trailing flowers.

My sketchbook is filled
with pictures of more inspired dances,
the ones held outdoors
where the men move like warriors
and the women sway
like trees
in a dream.

There is a dance with masks
that make the men look like lions

and one with horned headdresses
and another with graceful parasols
made of palm leaves.

My sketchbook is bursting
with stories
told by dances,
stories about life on two shores . . .
two distant lands,
Africa and Cuba,
joined and also separated
by the endless flow
of ocean waves
that sound
like music. . . .

CECILIA

When we visit the homes of free blacks
out in the countryside,
Fredrika keeps asking
a thousand questions
about their daily life.

Together, we listen to the tale
of an old man who rescued
his owner's children
during a slave rebellion
on another island.

He rowed a small boat
all the way to Cuba
where he lived as a free man,
working for wages

and caring for the children
he raised as his own.

Now, the two boys are grown
and they take care of him,
and together
all of them wonder
why the ability to share freedom
is such a rare
and fragile gift.

They tell me they do not believe
that people are either
black or white —
if that were so, then mixed-race children
would all be gray
instead of a myriad
lovely warm shades
of natural brown.

ELENA

I sit alone in my room
at the ornately barred window,
embroidering curlicues
like the fancy ironwork
that separates me
from the rest of the world.

I watch as my needle pierces
soft cloth.
The movement of the needle
helps my mind move back and forth
between many thoughts.

Why should a woman like Fredrika
have to choose between a career and love?
She would make such a good wife
and mother, if only she lived

in some distant future
when women will be free
to do more with their lives
than just sit behind bars,
embroidering cloth
for a hope chest that brings
no hope.

CECILIA

For the first time, Elena sneaks out
to help us rescue *cocuyos*.

Dogs and goats follow Fredrika
while she ransoms captive fireflies
and turns them loose.
Elena tells Fredrika that animals
follow her because she feeds them
from her bag of bananas and cookies,
but Fredrika insists
that friendly creatures follow her
simply because they know
that she believes
all animals have souls.

Without even trying to be a teacher,
Fredrika is teaching us,

showing us how to see things in new ways
instead of always thinking
the same old tired thoughts
that have been passed along by strangers
day after day, year after year
without any spirit of amazement
or wonder.

ELENA

I embroider until my eyes turn red.
I sew with excitement and energy.
My fingers hurt, and my shoulders ache
from bending over my embroidery hoop,
pretending to feel great enthusiasm
for my hope chest.

Mamá is delighted.
She had worried that I might
become lazy
as the year of my marriage
grows closer.

If she knew my secret plan,
she would slap me, or weep.
Fredrika will soon know my plan.
I need her help.

We must work together.
She cannot refuse.

Poor deluded Mamá.
She loves me, but her dreams
and mine are like two islands
separated by the waves
of a deep sea.

FREDRIKA

I won't be in Cuba much longer.
There was a time when I imagined
that I would be happy
living in any land
blessed with winter sun,
but now I know
that even though I still think of this island
as one of the outer courts of Paradise —
an Eden of natural beauty —
I could not bear to stay here
in the presence of slavery's
dreadful sadness.

Isn't life sorrowful enough
in places without slavery,
where so many men
treat the women

of their own families
like possessions of wood or stone,
useful objects
without souls?

E L E N A

Each embroidery stitch feels
like a step,
as if I am walking outdoors
in sunlight.

To buy more cloth and thread,
I ride in the swift *volanta* carriage
with Mamá.
She makes me sit up front
right behind Beni and his horse—
in the *niña bonita* seat—the "pretty girl" seat
where rich men can see me
and fall in love.

Mamá does not allow me
to set foot on the street

where my satin shoes
would get dirty.

So we stay in the carriage
while shopkeepers rush out
with an array of silver trays
bearing samples
of colorful fabrics
for us to see
and touch.

I choose silk
that feels like water
and linen that looks
like morning light
and satin as shiny as stars
and an exotic cloth
with sparkly threads
that make me think
of fireflies.

I ask Mamá to let me buy
pearls and jewels
so I can sew them into the centers
of all my embroidered flowers.

She is thrilled at the chance
to spend money so freely,
buying luxuries
the way other people
buy precious handfuls
of beans and rice.

CECILIA

Elena tells me she has a secret plan.
I have no idea what she means,
and she will not explain.
She knows I cannot read,
so she reads out loud from her journal
where she has written about Fredrika,
who told her that if she owns slaves
when she grows up
she will always have to live
with the temptation
of taking out her temper
on those who do her no harm.

Elena is rich, so I cannot imagine
how she could ever avoid
owning slaves.

She would have to run away with a poor man
and live in a hut, sweeping the dirt floor
and hoeing weeds
in a garden of wildflowers
and hunger.

ELENA

Today I will explain
my thrilling plan
to dear Fredrika,
and I will boldly
ask her to help.

I wonder what she talks about
when she is alone with Cecilia
wandering outdoors so freely
like men
or boys?

Do they know that I feel
like I could go mad
cooped up in this house
like a songbird
in a cage?

Am I selfish
to long for the freedom
to explore?

Shouldn't I just be thinking
about helping Cecilia
who has no freedom
at all?

FREDRIKA

Elena's idea
is enchanting!

She has learned
how to dream
of a magical world
without masters
and slaves.

If I can help her,
and if this plan works,
then I will finally
be able to leave Cuba
with new faith
in the future
of all women,
all girls . . .

BENI

I am surprised by the friendliness
of the foreign lady.

No free person has ever treated me
like an equal.

Even the freed slaves
keep their distance.

Fredrika stands beside the carriage
and talks to me,
as if I were a neighbor
instead of a servant,
while Cecilia translates
with a smile on her face.

Fredrika tells me that when she was young
her family took a grand tour of Europe,
riding all over France and Italy in a carriage.

When the carriage got stuck in deep mud,
she was not permitted to get out.

She had to stay inside, in the heat,
bored and sweaty,
simply because her mother
did not want her to speak
to the kind of people
who live in small houses
and walk
or ride swaybacked mules
on quiet country roads,
looking happy.

FREDRIKA

I am so excited
about Elena's ingenious plan
that it is hard for me
to keep the wonderful secret,
but I know that somehow
I must.

I show Beni my sketchbook.
The drawings are simple.
I am not a good artist.
I simply sketch to fix the images
in my mind
so that, later, I can write them
and bring them back to life.

Beni smiles when he sees
that Cecilia and Elena

have taken turns
sketching each other,
filling many pages of my notebook
with dreams and wishes
of their own.

Beni says he is amazed
that they have managed to learn
how to see each other
as friends.

CECILIA

Each time Elena speaks
of her secret plan,
I grow quiet.

Will I be blamed
for sharing
her daydreams
even though I do not know
what they are?

We take turns sketching
the view from her window.

Freedom is a wall. I cannot climb it.
Once my mind begins to picture liberty,
I am like Fredrika with her sketchbook,
frenzied, unaware of anything around her

beyond that one little paradise,
a single hut, with a few trees
and children at play
pretending that green leaves
are wings.

FREDRIKA

Elena's marvelous plan
is changing her
from the inside out.

She no longer wears
the pasty white makeup
that causes so many Cuban ladies
to look ghostly.

Her natural skin color
is the hue of wheat, the color
of men and women from southern Spain,
a land ruled by Moors
for seven hundred years.

Who will marry her
without her white makeup?

What will she be
without her parents'
illusions?

ELENA

I am finished.
My hope chest is full.
My plan will soon be complete.
Only Fredrika can help me now,
but I cannot tell her the real purpose
of my secret.
What will I do
if she refuses,
and what will happen
if my parents find out?
Will they blame Cecilia
even though
she is not involved
and knows nothing
about my scheme?

My mind soars
and whirls
in a dance
of wild fear
and graceful hope.

FREDRIKA

Helping Elena
makes me nervous,
but I struggle to stay calm
and confident.

Secrecy troubles me,
but how could this plan work
any other way?

Soon, I will leave Cuba,
and Elena will stay in her room,
embroidering flowers
over and over
like a poor farm girl
in a fairy tale,
spinning straw
into gold.

CECILIA

Secrecy
does not surprise me.

I am accustomed
to the hidden plans
of slaves.

There is always
one dream or another,
a scheme to escape
and flee
into the wilderness
to live
without chains.

Maps of the roads
to wild places

are the reason

that we are not allowed

to learn

how to read.

ELENA

My secret plan
is working.

Fredrika has helped me smuggle
all my lace and embroidery
out of the house,
one piece of cloth at a time.

As I placed the pillowcases
and shawls and collars and ruffles
in Fredrika's hands,
the folds of cloth stirred
in the sea breeze,
moving with a sigh
like wings.

FREDRIKA

On my last evening in Elena's home,
we climb up to the roof
to find shapes in clouds.

Cecilia is not with us.
She has an appointment,
so Elena and I have to depend
on our own ability to communicate
in a crazy mixture of English and Spanish
and the movements of our eyes
and our hands.

I believe we finally
understand each other
in our own mixed-up way.

CECILIA

I watch the fireflies in my mind
while I walk beneath a coppery sun
to the office
of the Magistrate.
My heart drums with gratitude.
My thoughts sing
with hope.

Fifteen gold dollars
was the amount Fredrika obtained
by selling all the fancy pearl-studded,
jewel-encrusted, lace-edged, ruffled folds
of embroidered cloth
that I thought Elena was keeping
for her own hope chest
so she could run away
and elope.

I assumed she was in love,
but as it turns out
her love was meant
for my child.
Fifteen gold dollars
is the price of liberty
for an unborn baby,
my baby,
a gift
so amazing,
the future,
this hope
I can share!

FREDRIKA

I think of the ladies in Europe
drinking hot tea with sugar.

Do they ever wonder
about the slaves
who chop the cane
that sweetens their tea?

How will they know
unless someone travels
and writes
about the tales
told by brave children
like Elena
and courageous mothers
like Cecilia?

E L E N A

The hope chest is empty now,
but tonight I will begin
to fill it again.

I will stitch new flowers
beneath the moon
that shines in
through my window,
flying past the bars
along with fireflies
and hope.

I no longer cover my head.
I think of the moonlight
as friendly
and safe.

HISTORICAL NOTE

Fredrika Bremer (1801–1865) was Sweden's first woman novelist and one of the world's earliest advocates of equal rights for women. Her travel books and stories about the daily lives of ordinary women influenced Victorian English literature and helped obtain partial voting rights for Swedish women as early as the 1860s. In 1854, deeply troubled by the Crimean War, Bremer published a historic peace document in newspapers all over the world, imploring women of all countries to unite in praying for peace and actively caring for the sick and the poor, especially children.

Bremer's Cuban letters, diaries, and sketches from her three-month visit in 1851 comprise the most complete known record of rural daily life on the island at that time. She described Cecilia, her young African-born translator, with admiration, affection, and concern. Together, they roamed the countryside, interviewing

slaves, free blacks, and poor whites. During school visits, Bremer argued in favor of equal education for girls.
In church, she kneeled in back, with the slaves.

Inspired by Bremer's poetic descriptions of tropical
farms and winter sun, tens of thousands of Swedish
immigrants moved to Cuba. In Havana, on the corner
of Obrapía and Los Oficios, a plaque commemorates
Fredrika Bremer's Cuban journey.

AUTHOR'S NOTE

Nearly all the events described in this book are documented in Fredrika Bremer's letters and diaries, but Elena is a fictional character, and the hope chest is imaginary.

Cecilia's husband was mentioned but not named or described in Bremer's letters. I have chosen to call him Beni, and to imagine that he was a skilled horseman.

Bremer wrote that Cecilia was eight years old when she was taken to Cuba from Africa, and that she said she still missed her mother. I have imagined Cecilia's childhood memories and her emotional response to the weeks she spent with Fredrika roaming the countryside, visiting the homes of freed slaves, and rescuing fireflies.

ACKNOWLEDGMENTS

I thank God for winter sun, fireflies, and friendship.

I am grateful that women no longer have to choose between writing and marriage, thanks to the efforts of equal-rights advocates such as Fredrika Bremer, who encouraged girls to change the world by thinking independently.

As always, I am deeply grateful to my husband, Curtis, my son, Victor, and my daughter, Nicole.

Special thanks to Reka Simonsen for editing so gracefully and so powerfully, and to Robin Tordini, Tim Jones, Deirdre Hare Jacobson, and everyone else at Henry Holt and Company.

I am grateful to Dan and Peggy Dunklee of the Clovis Book Barn, and William Secrest at the Fresno Library for help with rare-book searches.

For encouragement and friendship, *mil gracias* to Julie Molina and Celina Bowen.

REFERENCES

Bremer, Fredrika. *New Sketches of Every-Day Life*. Translated by Mary Howitt. New York: Harper & Brothers, 1850.

———. *The Homes of the New World: Impressions of America*. Translated by Mary Howitt. New York: Harper & Brothers, 1858.

———. *Life in the Old World*. Translated by Mary Howitt. New York: T. B. Peterson & Brothers, 1860.

———. *Life, Letters, and Posthumous Works of Fredrika Bremer*. Edited by Charlotte Bremer. Translated by Frederick Milow and Emily Nonnen. New York: Hurd and Houghton, 1868.

———. *Cartas desde Cuba.* Traducción por Matilde Goulard de Westberg. Havana: Editorial Arte y Literatura, 1981.

Stendahl, Brita K. *The Education of a Self-Made Woman: Fredrika Bremer, 1801–1865.* Lewiston, NY: Edwin Mellen Press, 1984.